Be careful what you wish for, my dear!

THE DOG
Princess Fairy Tails

HarperCollinsPublishers

Library of Congress Cataloging-in-Publication Data is available.
ISBN-10: 0-06-078310-9 (trade bdg.) — ISBN-13: 978-0-06-078310-5 (trade bdg.)
ISBN-10: 0-06-078311-7 (lib. bdg.) — ISBN-13: 978-0-06-078311-2 (lib. bdg.)

Typography by Jeanne L. Hogle
1 2 3 4 5 6 7 8 9 10

First Edition

Once upon a time in The Dog kingdom . . .

there was a pampered puppy princess with cool jewels—and her very own pink limousine. She had everything she could ever wish for.

Well, almost everything.

I'm starring in my own fairy tale!

The only thing missing was a prince.

Where's my Prince of Pup?

Her mother, the Queen, said she'd throw a grand ball for all the royal dogs in the land. Surely the princess would meet her own special prince that night.

Everydog who's anydog will be there!

Just to be on the safe side, the princess called on her fairy dogmother. "Please, please, please send a handsome prince to the ball! I promise I'll never ask for anything ever again."

"Are you absolutely sure a prince is all you want?" her fairy dogmother asked. "Very well. Your wish is granted."

Be careful what you wish for, my dear!

The night of the grand ball, all the other princess pups began to arrive from kingdoms far and wide.

I never leave my palace without my lucky jeweled pillow!

Kiss, kiss, dah-lings!

Is there going to be cake?

I keep kissing this frog, but no luck yet!

They quickly became very best friends. And of course,
the other princesses were looking for a prince too.

So when the prince arrived, our princess realized her big mistake.

Her fairy dogmother had done just what she had promised, all right—EXACTLY what she had promised. She sent a prince.

With only one prince and so many princesses, it wasn't going to be much of a grand ball. What were they to do?

somepuppy *call for a prince?*

At first some of the princesses got their tails all in knots.

He's mine! All mine!

Come on, girls!

I saw him first!

Princess

Don't get into a catfight!

Some perfected the princess pout.

But then they realized . . .

Let's never argue again!

that there's no puppy love like puppy pal love.

So they told the prince to go fetch—
and the new best friends went back
to playing . . .

Want to play another game

of firefly tag?

until they were too tired to play anymore.

May I borrow that lucky pillow?

After all, princesses
need their beauty rest.

And a slumber party is much more fun than a silly old ball.

I'm dreaming of butterflies.

So thanks anyway, fairy dogmother, but you can keep your handsome prince.

These princesses have more important things to dream about.

Zzzzzz...

Like soccer!

princess Power!